Pudge Ate A Prophet

A Big Fish Tale

Written by Damon J. Taylor & Daniel Taylor

Illustrated by Damon J. Taylor

They called him Pudge. His real name was Otis, but even his mother called him Pudge. It was easy to see why. . . . Pudge was big. Very big.

When he was born, the doctor said, "He's big for his age." When he was one year old, nice ladies in the park said, "He's big for his age." When he went to school at Flipper Elementary, the principal said, "He's big for his age."

Pudge understood that he was very big, but he *didn't* understand why God had made him so large. "I'm too big to fit through small spaces," Pudge thought. "And I'm too big to swim under things. I wonder what God can do with somebody as big as I am?"

Most of the time, other fish were nice to Pudge.

Sure, they didn't choose him first for finball, and they often didn't invite him to sleepovers. But things like that weren't always so bad.

Other times, they were not very nice at all. "Let's play house," Lucy the orange fish would say. "Pudge—you be the house!" Then the other fish would laugh. Pudge wouldn't laugh, but no one seemed to notice.

And sometimes Lenny the blowfish would puff up his cheeks as big as he could and say, "Guess who I am?" Then he'd point his fin at Pudge.

The other fish would laugh. Pudge wouldn't laugh, but no one seemed to notice.

When Pudge didn't feel like laughing, he'd swim off by himself. That's how he met Jonah.

Jonah was a prophet.

A prophet is a person who speaks for God. But Jonah didn't want to do what God had planned for him. Instead, Jonah ran away.

Soon a big storm made the seas toss and turn. The boat began to rock. Then the boat began to roll. The captain was very worried. "How can this be?" he cried.

"It's because of me," Jonah thought. He told the captain he was running from God.

"If you throw me overboard, this storm will stop," Jonah said.

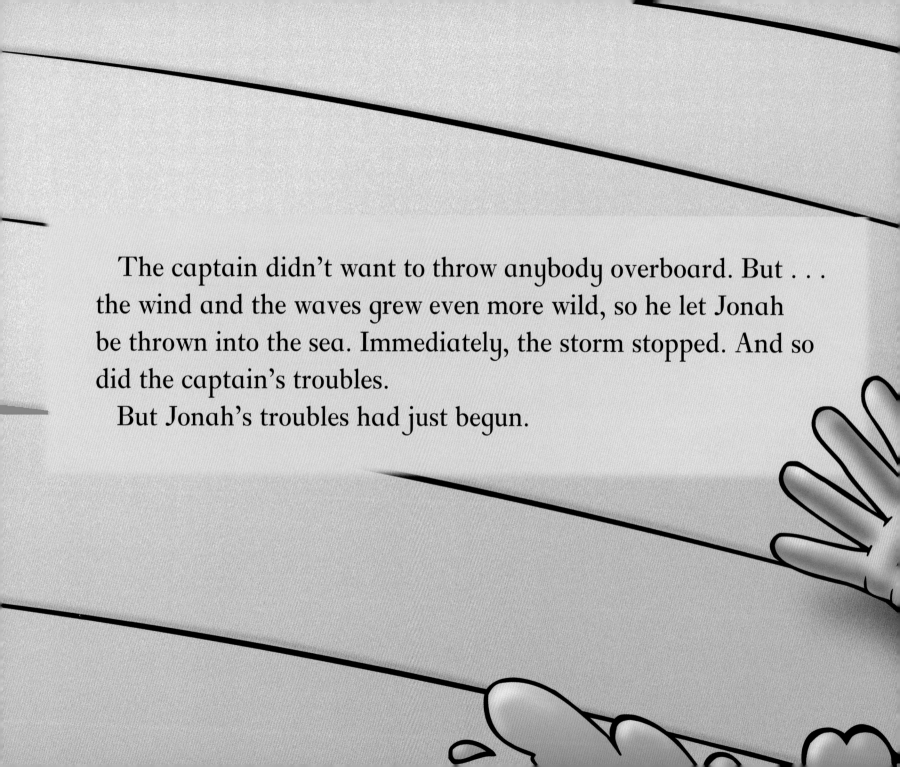

The captain didn't want to throw anybody overboard. But . . . the wind and the waves grew even more wild, so he let Jonah be thrown into the sea. Immediately, the storm stopped. And so did the captain's troubles.

But Jonah's troubles had just begun.

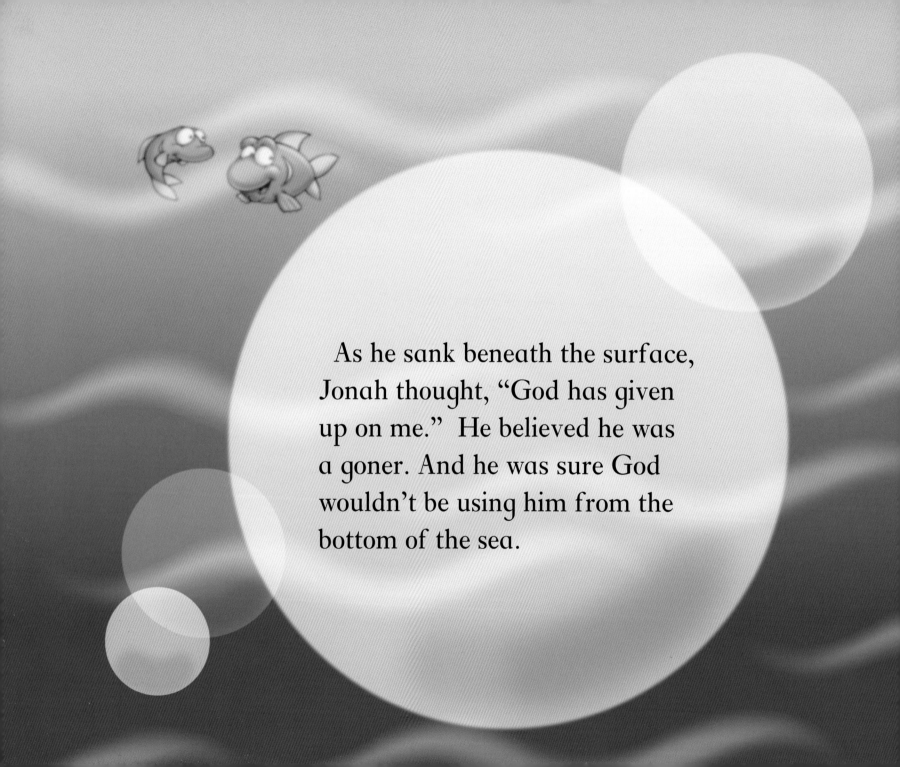

As he sank beneath the surface, Jonah thought, "God has given up on me." He believed he was a goner. And he was sure God wouldn't be using him from the bottom of the sea.

That's when Pudge ate Jonah.

After Pudge swallowed Jonah, Pudge heard a voice speak to him. It was God's voice.

Prophets like Jonah often heard God's voice. But for fish like Pudge, this was pretty rare. Pudge listened carefully.

"Pudge," God said, "I have an important mission for you. Hold my prophet in your tummy and swim to the shore of Nineveh. Then spit him out. Nineveh is about a three-day swim from here."

As Pudge swam toward Nineveh, he finally understood why God had made him so large. "I'm on an important mission for God!" This made Pudge feel good. "God knows I'm a good swimmer, and He made me big enough to hold a prophet!" This made Pudge feel *very* good.

Inside his belly, Pudge could hear Jonah praying, "I'm sorry, God. I want You to use me. Please forgive me."

For the next three days, Pudge and Jonah thought a lot about how God could use them. When they got to Nineveh, Pudge spat Jonah out onto dry land. . . . Jonah told the people God's message, and Pudge headed for home.

"Wow," thought Pudge, "God made me big enough to handle an important mission." Pudge knew that what he had done would help people. When Pudge thought about that, he smiled.

And that smile was big—very big.

THANKS PUDGE. YOU WERE A BIG HELP.

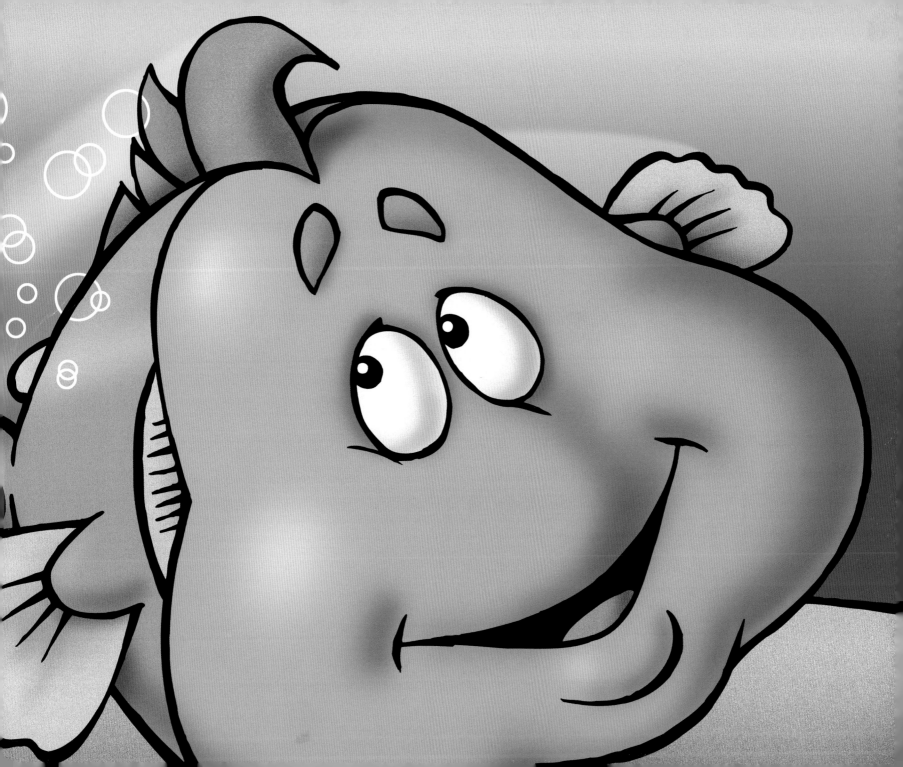

GOD HAD A PLAN FOR PUDGE AND JONAH. WHAT'S HIS PLAN FOR YOU?

For Parents

- Teach your children to enjoy their differences and employ their talents.
- Foster in them an excitement about how they were made.
- Help them learn to think about why God made them unique.

Being different is hard, especially for children. While classroom instruction focuses on "celebrating our differences," the same old thing happens on the playground. Without fail, someone is left alone, made fun of, or picked last for a game because of their looks, inability, or size.

   Whether your children are on the giving or receiving end of such treatment, Pudge's lesson is important. Being different just meant that God had made Pudge for a different part of His plan than He did the other fish. God picked Pudge for His team *because* of his difference, and He will do the same with all of us. Being a part of God's plan is exciting . . . no matter what part we play!

   Jonah had an important lesson to learn as well. God told him to take a message of hope to Nineveh. Jonah learned the hard way that we need to do whatever God asks of us.

   The questions below will help you dialogue with your children about how these important truths can be applied to their lives.

Discussion Questions:

- What is something about you that is different from other kids? Do other children make fun of your differences? Do you understand why God made you the way you are?
- Is there someone at your school who is different from you? How do you treat him or her? What is something you can do to help that child appreciate his or her differences?
- What is something you are really good at? Why are you good at it?
- On their three-day swim to Nineveh, Pudge and Jonah both thought about how God could use them. What are some ways God can use you to help accomplish His plan?